COYOTE

A TRICKSTER TALE FROM THE AMERICAN SOUTHWEST

TOLD AND ILLUSTRATED BY

Gerald McDermott

Houghton Mifflin Harcourt

Boston   New York

www.hmhco.com

The text of this book was set in Bryn Mawr.
The illustrations were done in gouache, colored pencil, and pastel on heavyweight cold-press watercolor paper.

The Library of Congress has cataloged the hardcover edition as follows:
McDermott, Gerald.
Coyote: a trickster tale from the American Southwest/told and illustrated by Gerald McDermott.
p. cm.
Summary: Coyote, who has a nose for trouble insists that the crows teach him how to fly, but the experience ends in disaster for him.
1. Indians of North America—Southwest. New—Legends. 2. Coyote (Legendary character)—Legends. [1. Coyote (Legendary character). 2. Indians of North America—Southwest, New—Legends.] 1. Title.
E78.S7M 136   1994
398.24'52974442—dc20
[E]   92-32979
ISBN 0- 15-220724-4
ISBN 0- 15-2201958-8 pb

Printed in China

SCP 35 34 33 32 31 30
4500691452

Coyote stories are the most widely known and most often told trickster tales of Native American tradition. From the Great Basin, to the Plains, to the pueblos of the Southwest, Coyote's misadventures have delighted and instructed for many centuries. His very name, *coyotl*, derives from Nahuatl, the ancient language of the Aztecs.

Stone Age hunters revered the coyote and tried to emulate the animal's cleverness and endurance. But for the Native American shepherds and planters of later ages, the coyote's conniving and thievery were a nuisance—and so he came to be mistrusted and vilified.

Coyote's image as a troublesome trickster, especially among the tribes of the Southwest, emerges in storytelling. He is portrayed as a devious, gluttonous fool, the perpetual victim of his own inquisitiveness. Coyote's insatiable desire to imitate others, to intrude on their lives, makes him seem very foolish . . . and very human.

The people of the Pueblo of Zuni, who excel in telling Coyote tales, assign a symbolic color to each of the world directions. They associate Coyote with the West and the color blue. In the present story—as in many Zuni tales of Coyote—he serves as an example of human vanity, and his misbehavior brings him misfortune.

—G. M.

For Jaycee, Joshua, and Alec

Coyote.

Blue Coyote.
He was going along, following his nose.
He had a nose for trouble.

Coyote stuck his nose into Badger's hole but got bitten.

Coyote wanted to have a flaming red head like Woodpecker, but his fur caught fire.

Coyote went looking for Snake
but only found trouble.

Coyote was always in trouble.

Coyote came to a place where
earth meets sky.
He heard laughing and singing.
He went up to take a look.

Coyote saw a flock of crows.
They were chanting.
They were dancing.

Then the birds spread their wings.
They flew through the air and circled the canyon.

"Oh, if only I could fly," said Coyote. "I would be the greatest coyote in all the world!"

Coyote called to the crows.
"Let me join you," he said.

"This foolish coyote wants to be like us,"
Old Man Crow said to his flock.
"Let's have some fun with him."

Old Man Crow turned one eye toward Coyote.
"You may dance with us," he said.

"Thank you! Thank you!" said Coyote.
"But I want to fly, too!"

"Maybe you can," said Old Man Crow.

Old Man Crow plucked a feather from his left wing.
He told his flock to do the same. They stuck the feathers in Coyote.
Coyote winced. His nose twitched.

The crows chuckled.

"You are ready to fly," said Old Man Crow.

The birds began their slow, steady chant. They hopped from one foot to the other. Coyote joined in the dance. Even though he got out of step and sang out of tune, he was very proud of himself.

The crows spread their wings and soared into the sky. Coyote followed. His flight was jerky. He tilted to one side. Since his feathers were only from the left wing of each bird, he was off balance.

He fell to the ground.

"Wait!" he cried out.
"Don't leave me behind!"

The birds returned and gathered round Coyote.

"We must balance him," said Old Man Crow.

Old Man Crow plucked a feather from his *right* wing.
Each of his flock did the same. Coyote cringed as they stuck
the feathers in his fur. The crows cackled.

"Now I'm perfect!" said Coyote. "I can fly as well as the rest of you."

Coyote had become rude and boastful.
He danced out of step.
He sang off-key.
The crows were no longer having fun.

The birds again began their slow, steady chant.
Coyote hopped along, flapping his feathered legs and
singing sour notes.
The dancers spread their wings and leapt into the air.

Soon the crows were flying high over the canyon.
Coyote struggled to keep up.

"Carry me!" he demanded.

The crows circled Coyote but didn't carry him.
Instead, they took back their feathers, one by one.

Coyote sank through the air.

He fell straight down.

"Wooooooooooooo!" he howled.

Coyote fell so fast, his tail caught fire.
He fell into a pool on the mesa.

Coyote crawled out of the water.
He heard laughter and saw the crows flying away.

Coyote ran after them.

He tripped and fell,
tumbling in the dirt.

Coyote went home soaked and covered with dust.
To this day, he is the color of dust.
To this day, his tail has a burnt, black tip.

To this day, Coyote still follows his nose.
He has a nose for trouble.
He always finds it.